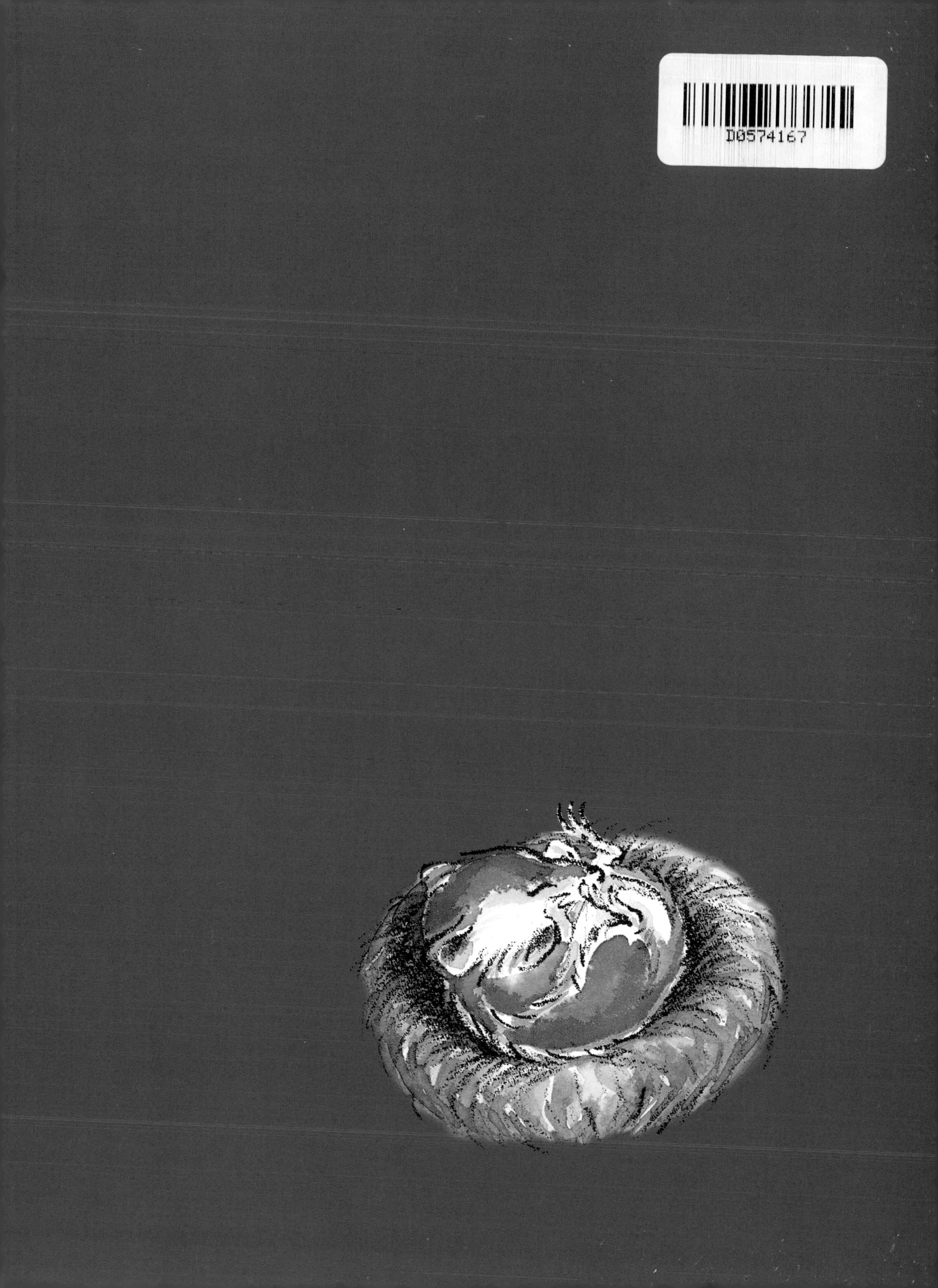
D0574167

First published in Switzerland under the title *Ich bin die stärkste Maus der Welt*

First published in the United States, Great Britain, Canada,
Australia, and New Zealand in 1998 by North-South Books,
an imprint of Nord-Süd Verlag AG, Gossau Zürich, Switzerland.

Library of Congress Cataloging-in-Publication Data is available.
A CIP catalogue record for this book is available from The British Library.
ISBN 1-55858-895-7 (trade binding)
1 3 5 7 9 TB 10 8 6 4 2
ISBN 1-55858-896-5 (library binding)
1 3 5 7 9 LB 10 8 6 4 2
Printed in Belgium

For more information about our books, and the authors and artists
who create them, visit our web site: http://www.northsouth.com

The Strongest Mouse in the World

By Udo Weigelt · Illustrated by Nicolas d'Aujourd'hui

Translated by J. Alison James

North-South Books · New York · London

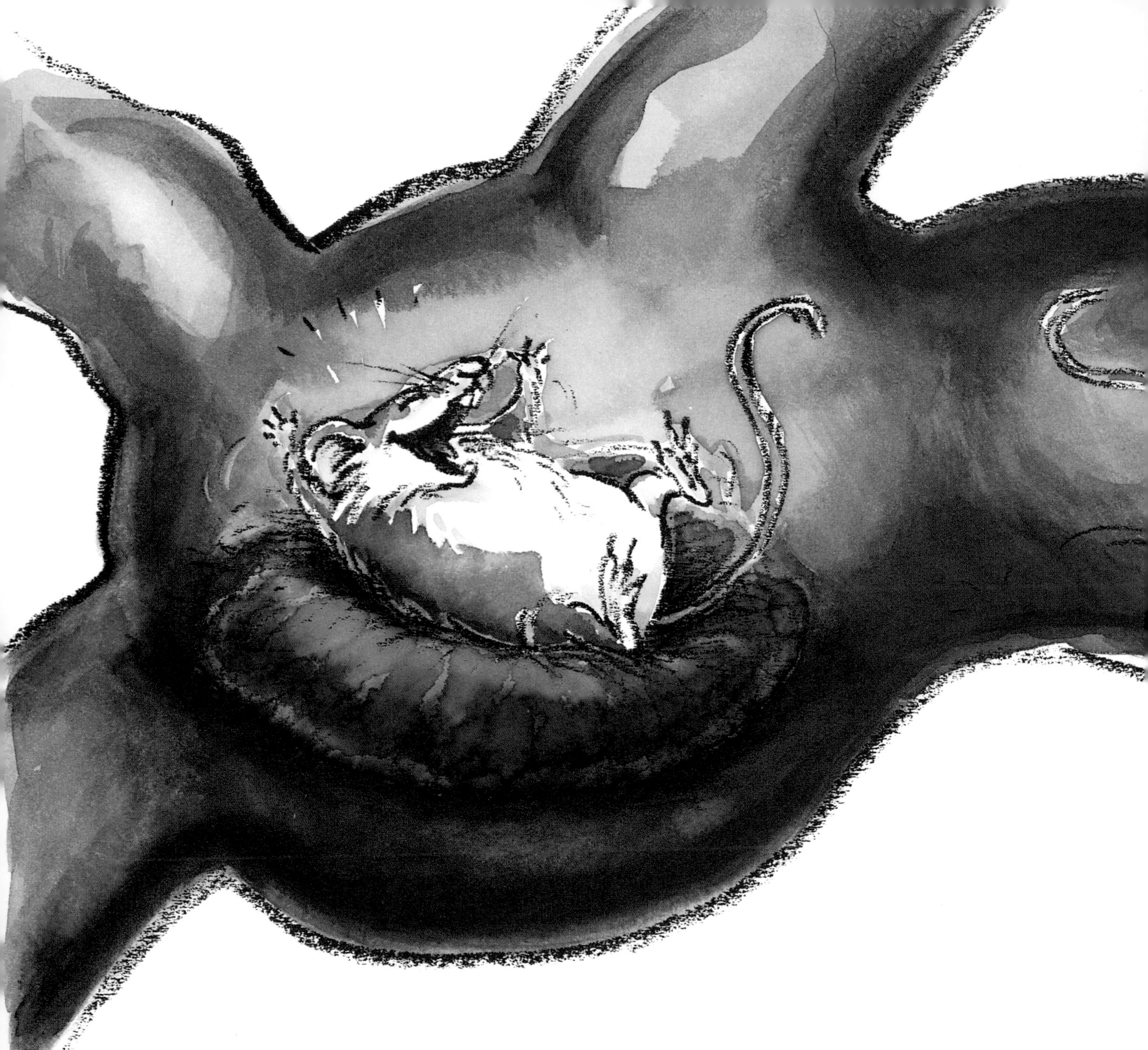

Lizzie the mouse woke up one morning feeling tremendous. She'd had a wonderful dream in which she had carried an incredibly heavy sack of nuts all the way across the forest and into her hole.

"Wow, if I can do that," she thought, "then I must be the strongest mouse in the world!" Lizzie sprang out of bed and bounded down to breakfast.

While she was gnawing her nuts, she said to herself: “I’m so strong, I could climb a tree! No, I’m so strong, I could run faster than a rabbit! No, I’m so strong, I could beat a bear!”

By the time she had finished eating, Lizzie had decided that she was the strongest animal in the entire woods, and so she hurried out to tell everyone.

"Good morning, Lizzie Mouse!" cried the hedgehog.

"Do you know what?" Lizzie said excitedly. "I am absolutely certain that I am the strongest animal in the entire woods!"

"But the strongest animal in the woods is surely Albert, the bear," the hedgehog said, surprised.

"Nope," said Lizzie. "I am. And I'll prove it. I'll wrestle that bear, and I'll throw him too."

"Maybe you should give it a try with me first?" offered the hedgehog.

"With you? Who could wrestle with you? You'd just roll yourself up into a spiky little ball."

Lizzie the mouse went on, leaving the astonished hedgehog behind.

Next Lizzie came across the mole. He was also quite surprised to hear what the mouse had to say. "Wouldn't you like to try wrestling me a bit first," he asked, "to find out if you really are that strong?"

"Nope," said Lizzie again. "You'll just throw sand in my face. I'll save myself for the bear. I'm trying to find him, but he has probably heard I'm coming and is hiding from me."

The mole couldn't quite imagine that, but he didn't say anything.

It was the same with the other animals that Lizzie the mouse met that morning. The fox, the badger, and the deer were all astonished by her boasting. But they had to admit that Lizzie was brave, wanting to wrestle the biggest and strongest animal in the woods.

Shortly after lunch, Lizzie got a visit from the squirrel.

"I'm supposed to tell you," said the squirrel, "that Albert the bear is waiting for you in the clearing — if you're really serious about wrestling him, that is. And all the other animals are going to watch."

"Of course I'm serious," said Lizzie, the Strongest Mouse in the World. "I'll be right there."

It was true. All the animals in the forest were waiting. And when Lizzie saw the bear, her first instinct was to run and hide. Suddenly she was not quite so sure that she was stronger than he was.

But of course she couldn't just run away now. So she pretended that nothing was wrong and began her stretching exercises to warm up. Still, Albert looked pretty ferocious, and Lizzie was a little bit afraid.

Then the fox, who was the referee, gave the signal to start.

The bear rose on his hind legs and roared.
Lizzie the mouse charged!

Lizzie seized the third claw of his right hind paw and tried to throw him off balance. She tugged and pulled and struggled and strained until . . .

with a sudden jolt Albert fell on his back.

Quick as a flash,
Lizzie jumped up on his belly.

"I won!" she cried. "I won!"

She had never felt so strong and proud in her life!
Then, suddenly, all the animals shouted:

"HAPPY BIRTHDAY,
LIZZIE!"

Lizzie had completely forgotten that it was her birthday! She thought for a minute, and looked at the bear, who was grinning at her in a goofy way. Then she looked carefully at his huge paws, each one much bigger than her entire body.

"Hey," asked Lizzie finally, "did you let me win?"

“Of course I did,” bellowed the bear cheerfully. “It’s your birthday, after all. I thought winning would make you happy.”

It certainly *had* made her happy. And so did the surprise party her friends threw for her. They stayed out singing and telling stories long into the night.

It was well after midnight when Lizzie made her way home. What a party that was! It was the very best birthday ever, she thought.

Exhausted, the mouse climbed back into her hole. But before she fell asleep, Lizzie smiled to herself, remembering how wonderful it had felt to whop that bear and to be the Strongest Mouse in the World!